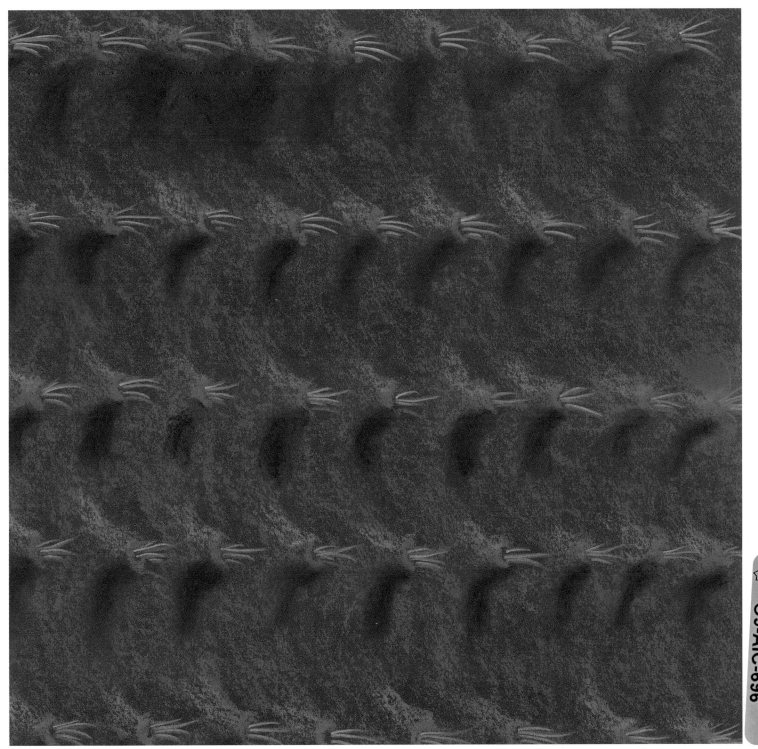

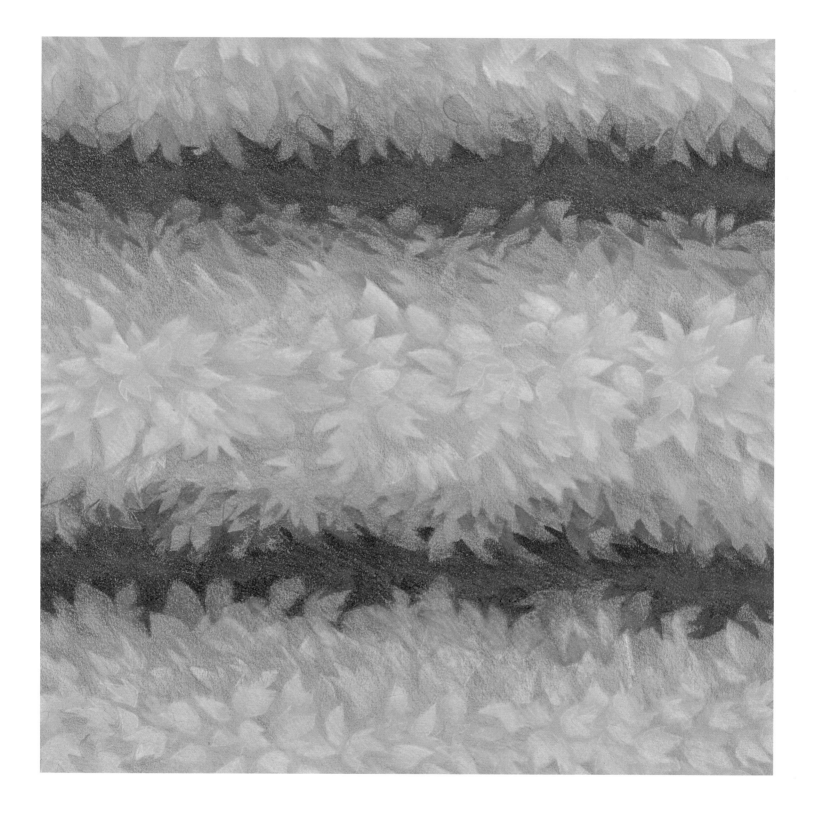

What a Wonderful Day to Be a Cow

by CAROLYN LESSER

illustrated by MELISSA BAY MATHIS

Dragonfly Books® Alfred A. Knopf • New York

The January wind howls around the barn, launching clouds of snow high into the air.

The shaggy farm dog loves the winter. He leaps and rolls in the snowdrifts like a circus acrobat. Tiny icicles sparkle on his muzzle, yet he is warm as toast in his furry coat.

What a wonderful day to be a farm dog.

On a dreary February day, the chicks huddle together. A warm light shines down on them like an indoor sun.

When the farmer pushes open the door, the chicks rush to a corner of the cozy coop, a stampede of yellow fluff on wiry feet.

What a wonderful day to be a chick.

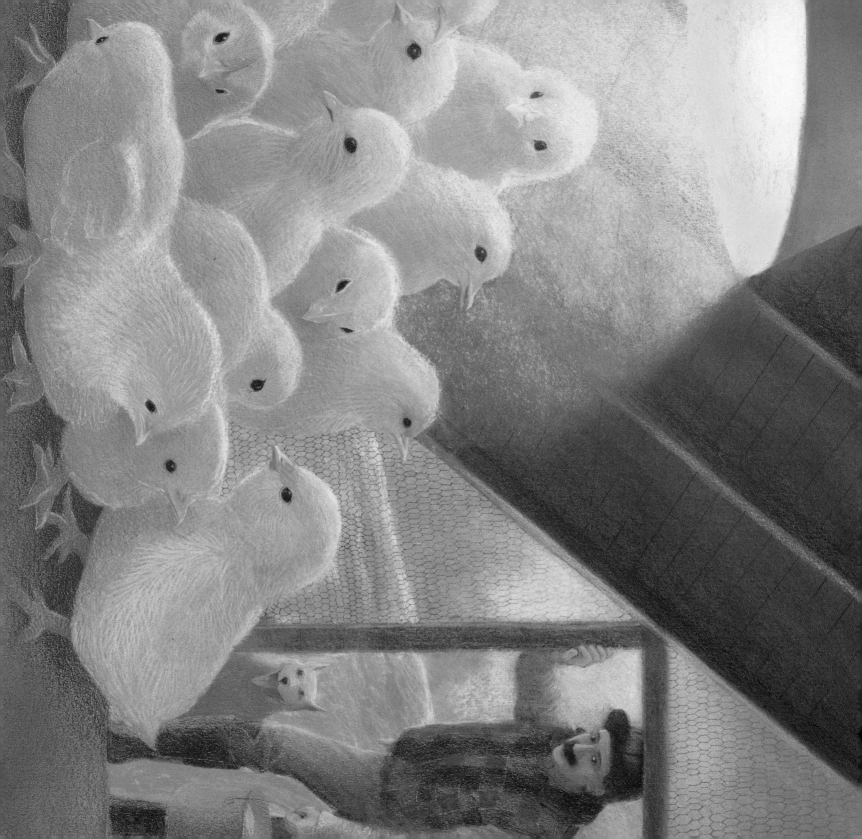

March fog rolls over the farm. High in the loft, a mother cat keeps her kittens. She feeds them, washes them, and tucks them into the sweet hay.

When her kittens are asleep in a purring heap, she prowls for mice like a shadow in the mist.

What a wonderful day to be a cat.

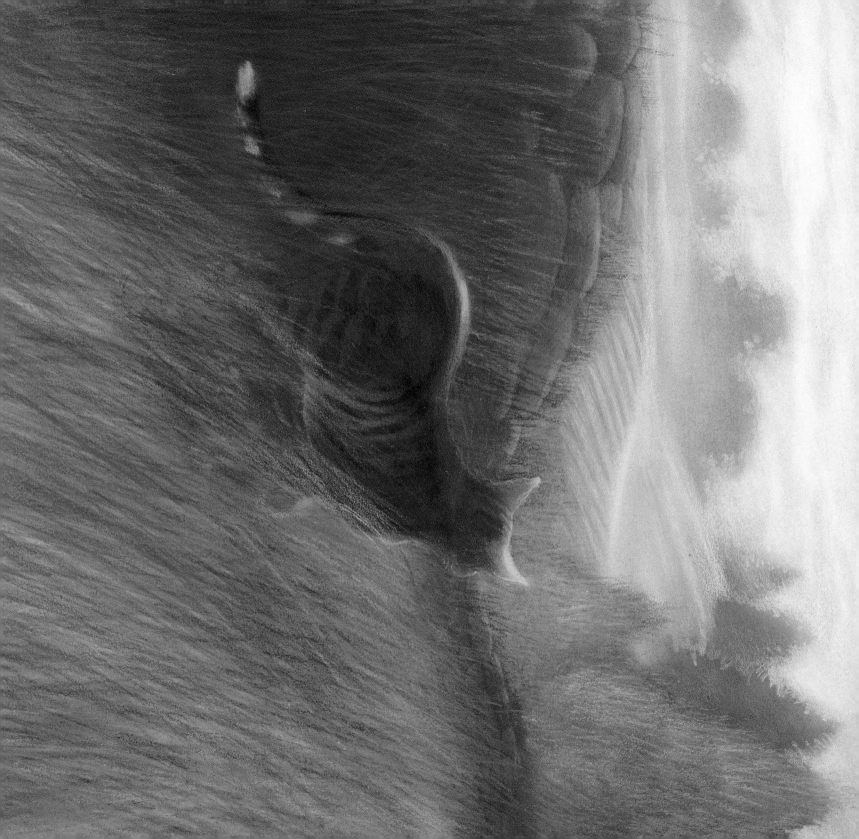

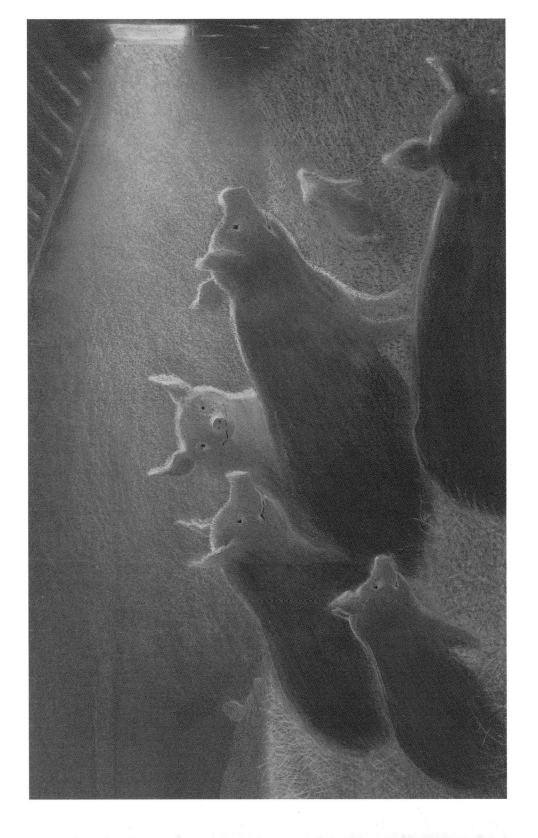

Rumbling thunder tumbles clouds in the April sky. Raindrops plop and splatter on the tin roof of the shed, waking the pile of pigs.

They wake and shake and push and shove, eager to get out into the oozy mud.

What a wonderful day to be a pig.

May sun warms the air as bluebirds warble. They swoop with weeds and grass to the branch of an old apple tree.

Blossoms nearly hide the nest. Their babies will be born in a tree of flowers, a garden in the sky.

What a wonderful day to be a bluebird.

In June, the sky is bluest-blue. Cows stroll lazily toward the pasture, twisting bright flowers into their mouths. Their calves sprint ahead. They zigzag through dandelions, showering silky seeds across the meadow.

Later, the cows drowse under a spreading oak, ears twitching, tails switching, swatting flies away.

What a wonderful day to be a cow.

On a crackling hot July afternoon, barn swallows glide out of the diamond-shaped window.

They plunge down, then skyrocket up again and again, like tiny kites on invisible strings.

What a wonderful day to be a barn swallow.

The fiery sun sinks in scorching August. Moths flutter around the barn lights as the evening choir begins.

Hundreds of hidden crickets chirp and trill. They fill the sizzling air with summer songs.

What a wonderful day to be a cricket.

The September night is cool. In the shed, wary mice slip past the cat, hunting for seeds and grain.

They dash from flowerpots to rusty buckets, scurrying across the stone floor like dry leaves blowing in the wind.

What a wonderful night to be a mouse.

October's frost is on the pasture. The horses prance, lifting their heads and tossing their manes. They trot crisply back and forth along the fence.

The wind of fall blows colder. The horses run, their long tails flying out behind them.

What a wonderful day to be a horse.

In November, there is always a chill of snow in the air, often a blanket of snow on the ground.

The red-tailed hawk flies high over the farm. He floats in wide circles on strong wings, searching for his dinner.

What a wonderful day to be a hawk.

December sends the animals into the barn to escape the cold. The chicks are now hens, roosting in the hayloft. Mice hide in tiny places, out of reach, for the kittens now are cats.

The pigs have traded mud for warm straw in their indoor pen. The cows stand patiently in their stalls, softly mooing. When the horses go out on sunny days, their breath makes fat clouds in front of their faces.

Like the bluebirds, the swallows have gone south. The whole farm misses their elegant air show. Only the hawk still flies from the woodland, ever watchful.

The barn is a sturdy ship sailing on billows of snow, keeping the animals warm and snug and safe until spring.

What a wonderful thing it is to live on a farm all the days of the year.

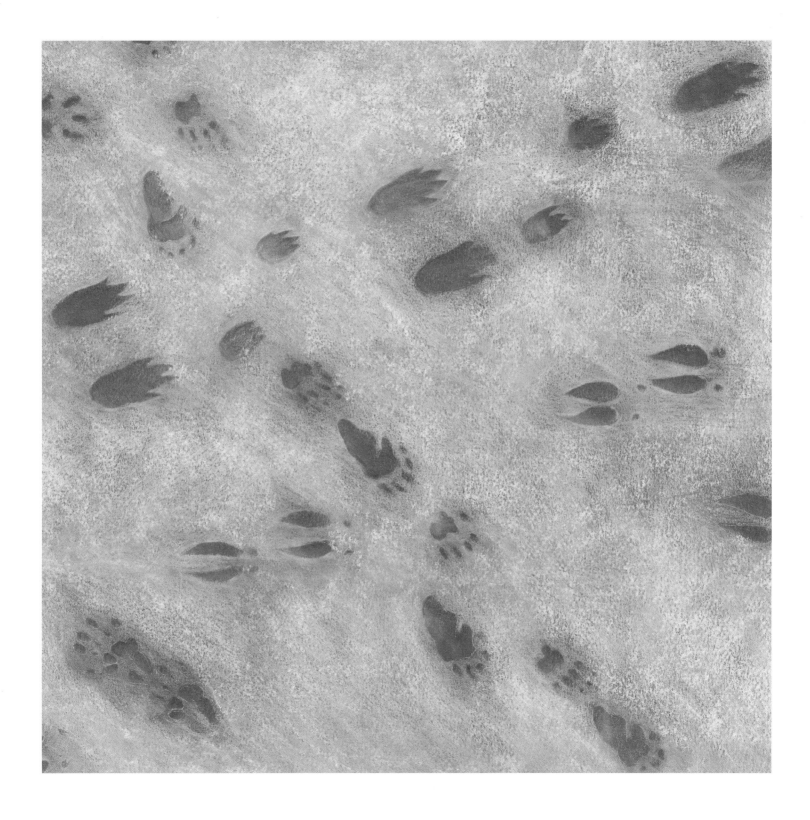

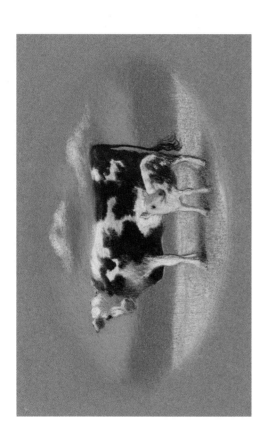

For my wonderful children—
Anne, Christopher, Michael, and Peter
With love

With thanks to my godmothers—Rene Qually, for love and faith,
and Irene Abitz, for love and the farm
—C.L.

For Eric, who had his own herd of cows as a boy—
and is now especially good with monkeys
—M.B.M.

DRAGONFLY BOOKS® PUBLISHED BY ALFRED A. KNOPF, INC.

Text copyright © 1995 by Carolyn Lesser. Illustrations copyright © 1995 by Melissa Bay Mathis.
All rights reserved under International and Pan-American Copyright Conventions.
Published in the United States by Alfred A. Knopf, Inc., New York, and simultaneously in Canada
by Random House of Canada Limited, Toronto. Distributed by Random House, Inc., New York.
Originally published in hardcover as a Borzoi Book by Alfred A. Knopf, Inc., in 1995.

www.randomhouse.com/kids

Library of Congress Cataloging-in-Publication Data
Lesser, Carolyn. What a wonderful day to be a cow / by Carolyn Lesser ; illustrated by Melissa Bay Mathis.
p.   cm.
Summary: Every month of the year, the animals on the farm enjoy their way of life and the weather that greets them.
[1. Domestic animals—Fiction. 2. Months—Fiction.]
I. Mathis, Melissa Bay, ill. II. Title.
PZ7.L562834Wh   1995   [E]—dc20   93-13211

ISBN 0-375-80212-6 (pbk.)

Printed in Singapore
10 9 8 7 6 5 4 3 2 1

First Dragonfly Books® edition: August 1999

DRAGONFLY BOOKS is a registered trademark of Alfred A. Knopf, Inc.